# MINNIE'S
# YOM KIPPUR BIRTHDAY

by
## Marilyn Singer

Pictures by
## Ruth Rosner

*Harper & Row, Publishers*

*To Max, Natasha, Bob and Laura Aronson*

*M.S.*

*For Tony, who sees the usual in a special way
and who knows about different birthdays.*

*R.R.*

ACKNOWLEDGMENTS

*Much thanks to Rabbi Dena Feingold,
Liz Gordon, Leslie Kimmelman, Roni Schotter,
Caryn Wiener, the Bank Street Writers Lab,
and most especially to my dear friend,
Steve Aronson, without whom I could not
have written this book.—M.S.*

Minnie's Yom Kippur Birthday
Text copyright © 1989 by Marilyn Singer
Illustrations copyright © 1989 by Ruth Rosner
Printed in the U.S.A. All rights reserved.
1  2  3  4  5  6  7  8  9  10

First Edition

Library of Congress Cataloging-in-Publication Data
Singer, Marilyn.
    Minnie's Yom Kippur birthday / by Marilyn Singer ; pictures by
Ruth Rosner. — 1st ed.
        p.    cm.
    Summary: When Minnie's birthday falls on Yom Kippur one year, she
wonders just what kind of birthday celebration she will have.
    ISBN 0-06-025846-2 : $
    ISBN 0-06-025847-0 (lib. bdg.) : $
    [1. Yom Kippur—Fiction.    2. Fasts and feasts—Judaism—Fiction.
3. Birthdays—Fiction.]    I. Rosner, Ruth, ill.    II. Title.
PZ7.S6172Mi  1989                                          88-14193
[E]—dc19                                                          CIP
                                                                   AC

Dad says I was born on a special day—
Rosh Hashanah, the Jewish New Year. He calls me
his New Year's baby.

Rosh Hashanah is on a different date every year,
like Thanksgiving or Easter. So I've really only been
a New Year's baby once.

But this year my birthday's on another special
day. It's called Yom Kippur, the Day of Atonement.
I don't know exactly what "Day of Atonement"
means. Dad says it's the most serious Jewish holiday
of all.

He says that my birthday this year is going to
be a little different, that we're not going to celebrate
it the way we usually do. But he tells me it's going
to be wonderful in its own way.

I wonder what he means.

If my birthday were on Thanksgiving, I know just what we'd do. Mom would take me to the zoo while Dad stayed home and made the turkey.

If it were on the Fourth of July, we'd all go on a picnic, then watch the fireworks when it got dark.

But my birthday is on Yom Kippur, and I'm not sure what we'll do.

Maybe Mom and Dad will make me a big party, and all my friends will come. There'll be fudge cake with five candles stuck in holders shaped like whales. We'll play games and get prizes. Mom will tell fortunes. Dad will dance. That would be a wonderful way to celebrate my birthday.

But Dad says Yom Kippur is serious. So I don't know if that's exactly what will happen.

I think about the party as I go to my room. My little sister Lucy is there, playing with my favorite doll. She won't give it back to me.

"My birthday's on Yom Kippur, the most special day of special days," I tell her. "And I'm going to have the most special birthday of all."

"I wish *my* birthday was on Yom Kippur," Lucy says. "Then I'd be special too."

"Well, it isn't, and you're not," I reply. "And give me back my doll." I snatch it away from her.

Lucy starts to cry.

I go to my older brother Arnold's room. He's working on a model train. I ask him to play Go Fish with me, but he says he's too busy.

"My birthday's on Yom Kippur," I tell him. "I'm going to do something wonderful, like going to the amusement park or the zoo or having a great big party."

Arnold looks at me. "I wouldn't count on that, Minnie. On Yom Kippur, you have to sit still and think about all the things you've done wrong during the year."

"You're a liar!" I yell. "You're just making that up."

Arnold shakes his head and goes back to his train.

I stick my tongue out at him and leave the room.

I run to my mother, who is sitting in the kitchen. "Arnold said on Yom Kippur we have to sit still all day and think about the bad things we've done. Is that true?"

"Well, not *all* day," answers Mom. "But Yom Kippur is the day we set aside to become a better person."

"Well, what kind of birthday will I have on a day like that?" I ask.

"It's a surprise," Mom says. "And I bet it will be terrific."

She makes me feel better. I can't wait for Yom Kippur and my birthday to come.

A week goes by. It's Yom Kippur. It's my birthday! I wake up singing, jump out of bed, wash, and put on my best dress. It is blue with a big white sash.

Then I hurry downstairs for breakfast. I hope Mom's making something good.

My whole family is in the kitchen. They're all dressed up too. "Happy birthday, Minnie," they all say.

But they don't give me any presents.

"On Yom Kippur," Mom tells me, "Dad and I fast. That means we don't eat. Arnold is going to fast too. You and Lucy don't have to, but I can't make you any special food."

She hands me a bowl of corn flakes.

I eat it very slowly.

Just when I finish eating, the doorbell rings. "I'll
get it," I say.

When I open the front door, Judy, the baby-
sitter, is standing there. "Happy birthday, Minnie,"
she greets me.

"Thank you," I answer. I don't know why she's
here on my birthday. But then I figure it out. Mom
and Dad have made me a party and Judy's my first
guest. "I'm happy you could come," I tell her, the
way you're supposed to.

She smiles and follows me into the kitchen. "Hello, Mr. and Mrs. Hirsh," she says to Mom and Dad. "I hope I'm not too early."

"No, not at all." Mom smiles.

I wait for her to tell me about the party.

Instead she says, "Judy's going to stay with you and Lucy while Dad, Arnold, and I go to Temple. Be good. We'll see you later."

I frown as I watch them leave. I've never been to Temple, but I know what it is because Arnold told me. It's a place where people go to sing and pray. I wish I could go and see it myself.

"I bet you're having a really different birthday this year," Judy remarks.

"It's different all right," I grumble.

Mom and Dad and Arnold are gone a long time. Judy reads Lucy and me two stories. They are boring. Then we play three games of Go Fish. I lose all of them.

I'm feeling bad.

Finally Mom, Dad, and Arnold come back and Judy leaves. "We're going to rest until later this afternoon," Dad tells me. "Then we'll *all* go to Temple."

"Yippee!" I shout. I'm going to Temple after all—for the very first time. I'm going to sing and pray and have lots of fun. What a special birthday!

I comb my hair and straighten my sash. Then I sit quietly until Mom and Dad are ready to go. It takes them a long time.

"Okay, Minnie," Dad says at last. "Put on your coat."

I put on my coat, and we all leave together. We

drive until we get to a big building with big doors and a lot of windows. The windows have stars on them. So do the doors.

Inside, there are lots of people in the hall, standing around and talking to each other. They're all dressed up and most of them are holding books. Finally everyone goes into a big, bright room with rows and rows of seats. I see my friends Laura and Susie and other people I know. But they don't see

me. They're looking at the stage in front of the
room. At the back of the stage is a big, fancy closet.
It has a golden light hanging over it and a thin
curtain, with something all white and silver spar-
kling behind it.

I sit down between Arnold and Lucy. "What's that thing?" I whisper to Arnold, pointing at the closet.

"That's the ark with the Torah inside. The Torah is the book of Jewish teaching," he whispers back.

"Why is there a light there?"

"That's the eternal light. It burns forever and ever."

"You mean it never goes out?"

"That's right."

"How can it do that?"

"Shh," Mom says. "In Temple, you must be quiet."

I stop talking. But I keep thinking about the light.

Then two people come out. One is a short man.
The other is a tall woman. The man has a beard.
The woman has bright red hair. They both are wear-
ing white robes, white shawls, and little white hats
like Dad and Arnold have on. They stand on the
stage behind high, skinny desks, and the woman
starts to sing.

"That's the cantor," Arnold whispers.

"She has a pretty voice," says Lucy.

I like her voice too. But I can't understand the words.

"She's singing in Hebrew," Arnold explains.

The cantor sings for a long time. After a while, we all stand up. A lot of people sing along with her. Mom, Dad, and Arnold do too. Then everybody sits down.

And the man starts talking.

"That's the rabbi," Arnold tells me.

At first I can't understand him either. He says things in Hebrew. People read back to him out of their books. We stand up and sit down a lot.

Finally, when everyone is seated, the rabbi looks at us and tells a story. It's about a man named Jonah who did something wrong and got swallowed by a whale. When he told God he was sorry, he got spit right out.

I don't like the story. And I feel so bad I want to cry.

Temple isn't so much fun after all. And this birthday isn't wonderful at all. This birthday is the most terrible birthday I've ever had.

Then the rabbi says, "Children, today is Yom Kippur. It is a very special day. It is the holiest day of our year, the Day of Atonement. On this day you must think about what kind of person you've been and how you can become better. You must remember the things you're sorry for and apologize for them, just as Jonah did. Then God will forgive you, as God forgave Jonah. That's what it means to atone."

He talks some more, but I'm not listening. I'm thinking about how I must've done something really bad to make God mad and give me such a terrible birthday.

But I can't remember what it was.

Then I hear the rabbi say, "Most people don't do big bad things like Jonah did to God, but little bad things to other people. They're the hardest of all to remember. But if you think hard, they'll come back to you. And when they do, you must apologize as soon as possible to the people you've hurt."

He stops talking, and the cantor begins to sing again.

I think and think—and suddenly, I remember.
I told Lucy she wasn't special.
I called Arnold a liar.
I want to apologize to them right away.
"Lucy," I whisper, "I'm sorry I said you weren't special. I was just being mean."
Lucy smiles at me.
"Arnold," I say in a low voice, "I'm sorry I called you a liar. You're not. Everything you said is true."
"Shh," says Arnold, but he pats my back.
And then I don't feel so bad anymore. I feel like I did something good.

I look at the stage. The cantor is taking out a funny-looking horn.

"This is the shofar, the ram's horn," the rabbi says. "Since long ago, it has been used to call people together for war or peace, for prayer, for celebration. It is blown at Rosh Hashanah to remind us that we need to stop and think about the way we've led our lives. It is blown again now, at the end of Yom Kippur, to tell us the holiday is over and we should all rejoice."

The cantor blows the shofar. It is a loud, long, and happy sound. It makes me laugh.

We all stand up. The rabbi raises his hands into the air and blesses everyone. People turn to each other, shake hands, and wish "Happy New Year."

But we don't leave the Temple. Instead we go
down the hall to another room with a long table.
On the table are plates of good things to eat and
pitchers of good things to drink.

The rabbi announces, "Now that Yom Kippur
is over, we are going to do two things. We are going
to break our fast with this delicious food. In our
Temple, we do this every year." He says a prayer
over the food.

We all fill up our plates. We talk and laugh and have a good time, just like we're at a party.

When we're full of food, the rabbi says, "I said before we were going to do two things. We've already broken our fast. Now it's time for something we've never done before. Something very special." He looks across the room and calls, "Laura, Susie, are you ready?"

"Yes," they call back.

They come forward carrying a big cake—a fudge cake with five candles stuck in holders shaped like whales. And on the cake are three words: HAPPY BIRTHDAY, MINNIE.

"I told you this would be a different birthday," says Dad, giving me a hug.

"It's different all right," I agree with a big smile.

Then everybody sings "Happy Birthday" while I cut the cake.